The Little Engine That Could™

Goes on a CLASS TRIP

Written by Monique Z. Stephens
Based on the original story by Watty Piper

Illustrated by Jose Maria Cardona

Weekly Reader is a registered trademark of Weekly Reader Corporation
2007 Edition

Library of Congress control number: 2003005377

ISBN 0-448-43180-7

Printed in the United States of America

The Little Engine That Could was so excited. The kids in Piney Vale Elementary School's second-grade class were going on a trip to the safari zoo. And the Little Blue Engine was going with them!

"Hi, Little Engine!" the children cried as they climbed on board.

The Little Blue Engine tooted her horn happily.

When they arrived at the safari zoo, the zookeeper, Sally, came out to greet them.

"Ready to meet the animals?" she asked. The class cheered.

They visited the Monkey Forest. Apes and gorillas lumbered around and monkeys of all kinds swung from tree to tree. One naughty monkey even swiped their teacher Mr. Beasley's hat!

"Next stop, African Plains!" called Sally. The class oohed and ahhed to see so many wild animals grazing nearby. One tall giraffe even munched on leaves from a tree right above their heads!

Suddenly, one of the zoo workers drove up to them.

"Sally, I've been looking all over for you!" he cried. "Reba's baby Lulu wandered away from the herd. She's been missing for hours!"

Reba was a big gray elephant. Her baby Lulu was only a few days old.

Sally looked worried. "Baby Lulu will be frightened to be separated from her herd— she's never been away from her mother before. She might even get hurt!"

The children gasped.

"How are you going to find her?" asked one little boy.

Sally looked at the zoo worker. "Max, you take the jeep and search the south side of the park. I'll look for Lulu in the forest. Little Engine, do you think you can help us find her?"

The second graders looked at the Little Engine, holding their breath.

"Yes, I think I can," the Little Blue Engine answered. Sally nodded. "Good. Let's go!"

With Sally as her guide, the Little Engine chugged around the grassy field into a thick jungle of trees.

"Lulu! Lulu!" the schoolchildren called. They peered through the thick forest, but there was no sign of the baby elephant.

After the class had been searching the woods for over an hour, the zoo worker Max came driving up to them in his jeep.

"I've searched everywhere else in the park, and I'm sure Lulu's not there," Max told Sally. "She has to be somewhere in this forest."

Sally frowned. "That can only mean one thing: Lulu's scared and she's hiding!"

"We have to think of a way to draw Lulu out," Sally continued.

Everyone got quiet, thinking.

From way off in the distance came the faint sound of an elephant trumpeting. That gave the Little Engine an idea.

"I think I know how we can make Lulu come to us!" she said excitedly.

As everyone watched, the Little Engine That Could took a big breath. Then she blew her horn slowly, so that the sound came out deep and low. It sounded just like an elephant trumpeting!

"Good idea, Little Engine!" Sally cried. But would it work?

Just then Lulu came crashing through the trees. It worked!

The Little Engine That Could led Lulu out of the forest. The Little Blue Engine blew her horn, deep and low, and the baby elephant trumpeted back, all the way back to the elephant herd.

When Lulu saw her mother, she gave one last excited trumpet and bounded over to her.

The whole class cheered to see the baby reunited with her mother.

"Hurray for Little Engine!"

"We knew you could do it!" said Mr. Beasley. The Little Engine That Could blushed. But the teacher wasn't done.

He placed a gold star on the
Little Engine's chest. "For a job well done!"
The Little Engine couldn't have been
more proud!